HIGH-TECH NINJA HEROES

ADAPTED BY MICHAEL PETRANEK FROM THE SCREENPLAY

STORY BY HILARY WINSTON & BOB LOGAN & PAUL FISHER AND BOB LOGAN &
PAUL FISHER & WILLIAM WHEELER & TOM WHEELER

SCREENPLAY BY BOB LOGAN & PAUL FISHER & WILLIAM WHEELER &
TOM WHEELER AND JARED STERN & JOHN WHITTINGTON

SCHOLASTIC INC.

Adapted by Michael Petranek from the screenplay

Story by Hilary Winston & Bob Logan & Paul Fisher and Bob Logan & Paul Fisher & William Wheeler & Tom Wheeler

Screenplay by Bob Logan & Paul Fisher & William Wheeler & Tom Wheeler and Jared Stern & John Whittington

ISBN: 978-1-338-13968-6

10 9 8 7 6 5 4 3   17 18 19 20 21
Printed in the U.S.A.   40

First printing 2017
Book design by Jessica Meltzer

Greetings. I am Master Wu. I am here to tell you about my students, the Secret Ninja Force.

This is the story of how they defeated one enemy, but found a new challenge.

The Secret Ninja Force has six members — Lloyd, Nya, Cole, Jay, Kai, and Zane. They are high school students, and they also protect Ninjago City. They are very busy teenagers!

Ninjago City's biggest enemy is Lord Garmadon. Garmadon has four arms, red eyes, sharp teeth, and . . . he's my brother.

Most of our family get-togethers are not very fun.

Garmadon is the head of an army of Sharkmen. In truth, they are not actually Sharkmen . . . just men and women wearing shark suits. They can attack Ninjago City from the water.

Lloyd is the Green Ninja, and he leads the Secret Ninja Force. Lloyd builds all the ninja's mechs, too.

Garmadon is Lloyd's dad, but they are not very close. Garmadon pronounces his name wrong — he calls him "La-loyd." But the first *L* is supposed to be silent, like a ninja.

Koko is Lloyd's mother. She has always told Lloyd she and Garmadon worked in an office together before he decided to take over the world. He was much friendlier back then.

Kai and Nya are brother and sister. Kai is fearless and hotheaded, while Nya is one of the fiercest students I have ever taught.

Cole is another member of the ninja team. He loves music. His mech has an awesome sound system, and he loves making mixtapes. If you don't know what that is, ask an older person.

Jay is the Blue Ninja, and he is a great inventor. He loves to make jokes and is very hardworking.

Zane is a Nindroid who is always trying to fit in and crack jokes, but being a robot makes him a little different.

The ninja all have cool mechs that they use to fight anyone who invades Ninjago City . . .

. . . the mechs are neat, but it takes more than technology to be a true ninja. Ninja are sneaky. These mechs are very, very loud!

Recently, the ninja put their mechs to the test. Garmadon attacked Ninjago City for the hundredth time.

The ninja are very good at protecting the city, but sometimes they end up causing a lot of damage.

During the battle, Lloyd fell off his mech and landed in an apartment. He had to protect a baby while fighting some Sharkmen. He had his hands full!

The ninja defeated Garmadon and sent him back to his volcano lair.
"I'll be back," Garmadon vowed. "And when I return, I'll have something really wicked for you!"

I knew what Garmadon said was true. He would be back, and things would only get worse.

We returned to the ship where I train the ninja, the *Destiny's Bounty*.
Lloyd, Nya, Cole, Jay, Kai, and Zane were very happy they'd defeated Garmadon.

"Guys, that was awesome! Today we were so ninja!" Nya said.

But I had some things I needed to tell the ninja.

"There's nothing *ninja* about you," I said. "Ninja are supposed to be invisible! But you keep blowing everything up with your crazy machines!"

"Garmadon will be back, same as before," I said. "Someday you will come up against something your mechs cannot beat. It is time to truly become . . . ninja!"

I know the ninja were disappointed. They did not want to listen to me, but it was true. They needed to become *real* ninja. Not just crazy kids with wacky mechs.

So we began training. And it is here that you find us.

Garmadon will come back, and when he does, the ninja must find their inner strength and become true ninja. For that is the only way they will ever defeat him and save Ninjago City for good!

Copyright © 2017 Warner Bros. Entertainment Inc. & The LEGO Group.
THE LEGO NINJAGO MOVIE © & ™ Warner Bros. Entertainment Inc. & The LEGO Group. LEGO, the LEGO logo, the Minifigure, the Brick and Knob
configurations and NINJAGO are trademarks and/or copyrights of the LEGO Group. © 2017 The LEGO Group. All rights reserved. (s17)
ISBN: 978-1-338-13968-6

PO# 577458